This book is dedicated to my grandchildren
Isabel, Finn, Kailani and Maya
and children everywhere who love kittens.

Discussions points and exercices for children are available on relevant page of publisher website www.findhornpress.com

Diana Cooper is well known for her books on angels, fairies, unicorns and the spiritual world, all written from her own personal experiences. For more information about these subjects see her website www.dianacooper.com – *there is also a children's corner.*

If you wish to talk to someone about the subjects in this book, the Diana Cooper School website lists teachers throughout the world: www.dianacooperschool.com

Text © Diana Cooper 2011
Edited by Elaine Wood
Illustrations © Kate Shannon 2011
Interior design by Thierry Bogliolo

ISBN 978-1-84409-550-6

Printed in the European Union

Published by
Findhorn Press
117–121 High Street
Forres IV36 1PA
Scotland, UK

www.findhornpress.com

The Magical Adventures of Tara and the Talking Kitten

by Diana Cooper
illustrated by Kate Shannon

FINDHORN PRESS

Tara's birthday

It was Tara's birthday, her seventh birthday, which is why she remembered it so well. It was the day something extraordinary happened and everything changed. It was like a miracle. However, the day did not start well.

Tara wanted a party, but was not having one. Mum had said parties cost a fortune and they couldn't afford it, she had also said no one would want to come. Jack has a lot of friends and so has Mel, but Tara doesn't – her Mum says it is because she is horrid to everyone.

Jack is Tara's horrible little four year old brother (well he is quite nice sometimes) and Mel is her nine year old, goody-goody, butter-wouldn't-melt-in-your-mouth sister, with long fair hair in a pony tail and a giggling gang of friends.

Auntie Dottie and Granny were the only visitors Tara could expect today. Tara scowled and shrugged. "I don't like the girls at school and I didn't want a party anyway." Tara flounced

off to her room and slammed the door. Mum sighed.

It wasn't fair, Tara thought. She was different. Her hair was curly and messy. Her voice was too loud when she was excited and she never seemed to have a friend. And Mum was always cross with her.

Tara heard the door bell. She didn't dislike Auntie Dottie, but she was very fat and red faced. She also wore lots of perfume which suffocated you when she kissed you. Tara decided to try to be very good today. She ran down to the hall and stood by Mel and Jack, trying to stand like her sister. Dad opened the door and said heartily, "Hello Dottie, it's lovely to see you." Auntie Dottie wheezed and panted through the door. She was wearing a dress covered in red polka dots – the exact colour of her face – and carrying a huge handbag.

Mum frowned a warning at Tara – whose eyes had grown as big as saucers staring at her rather large auntie dressed in rather large polka dots – and so did Dad. But she couldn't help it.

The words just jumped out of her mouth without asking her brain first. Before Auntie Dottie had even had time to say, 'Happy birthday' Tara squealed "Spotty Dottie! Yuck!"

Dad, Mum and Mel scowled. Jack laughed. Auntie Dottie looked shocked.

"Say sorry at once!" commanded her parents with one voice.

"Sorry," she muttered so quietly they could hardly hear her.

"What a rude little girl! I brought you the singing doll you wanted for your birthday. Now I'm not going to give it to you." Auntie Dottie put the parcel behind her back and headed for the kitchen.

Tara shouted, "I hate you!" and ran up to her room howling. It wasn't fair, it was her birthday and it was exactly the doll she had wanted. She was cross with everyone – including herself.

Granny

It was about an hour later that Tara heard Auntie Dottie leave. She kicked the bed in a temper before skipping downstairs – pretending nothing had happened. The phone rang as she burst into the kitchen. It was Granny calling to say she had a special birthday gift for Tara, but she wanted to check with Mum and Dad first. Her parents took the phone into the sitting room and shut the door. Tara, Mel and Jack tiptoed to the door to try to hear but Dad had turned off the loudspeaker. All they heard was Dad say "No!" very loudly and Mum murmur something about it maybe doing the child good.

When her parents returned to the kitchen Dad looked a bit worried. Mum was smiling for once. But neither of them said a word. Tara knew she must be very, very good so she went into the garden and sat on the swing where she could not say or do anything wrong. Whatever could her present be?

When Granny arrived she was carrying a basket. She carefully placed it on the floor, wished Tara a "Very Happy Birthday" and opened the lid. Out jumped a small grey kitten. With its tail straight up in the air like a mast it ran over to Tara and looked at her with big green eyes. Tara beamed from ear to ear as she knelt down and picked it up. "Oh thank you Granny. It's the best present I've ever had."

She had no idea then just how special it was going to be. The magic started before lunch.

"Come and help me get lunch," Mum said to the others, "While Tara gets to know her kitten."

"You'll need to choose a name for him," said Dad, ushering the others out of the door.

"Call him Smoky," suggested Mel, "Because he's grey."

"Or Snot," added Jack, "Cos he's got green eyes." He paused. "If he was brown you could call him…." Dad grabbed him by the shoulder and pulled him out of the room. Granny smiled at Tara as she shut the door behind her.

My name is Ash-ting

Tara sat by the beautiful kitten who was looking at her with his head cocked to one side. "Would you like to be called Smoky?" she crooned.

Suddenly she felt as if something tapped her lightly on the forehead and she heard a voice say: *"No, I'm Ash-ting."*

Tara was silent with shock. The voice came again: *"My name is Ash-ting."*

"You can talk?" the little girl stared at her new kitten and croaked in surprise.

"Of course," responded the little grey ball of fluff. *"All animals can talk, but not everyone can hear them like you do."*

"Ash-ting," she repeated. "That's a funny name."

"You must never say that about a name," responded Ash-ting severely. *"Names are important. Ash is my colour and Ting is my dynasty."*

"What's a dynasty?"

"It's a family name."

Tara thought for a moment, then she smiled and her face lit up. "I think it's a beautiful name and I think you are beautiful, too."

She picked Ash-ting up and he snuggled into her arms purring as she carried him into the dining room for her very special birthday lunch.

Tara perched on one of the dining room chairs with the purring kitten on her knee. "His name is Ash-ting," she announced proudly.

"What a silly name," jeered Jack and she could sense the family tensing as they waited for her outburst.

"I think it's a pretty name," said Mum hastily.

"Where did you get that name from?" Granny asked.

But for once Tara did not rise to Jack's bait.

"Names are important," she told them all with dignity. "Ash is his colour and," she felt a thump between her eyes and looked at the kitten who was staring intently at her.

"Stop, Tara! You can't say Ting is my dynasty, they will not understand. Just say you like it."

Tara saw the sense of that. "And I just like Ting," she added airily.

"Very nice," said Dad, relieved a quarrel had been prevented. 'But you can't have Ash-ting at the table.'

She was opening her mouth to protest when the kitten said, *"Quite right! Say 'Yes Daddy' and put me in my basket please. I'm tired. I want to sleep."* He yawned, showing his pink tongue, and everyone said "Aaahhh."

"Yes Daddy," replied Tara and leapt up to put the kitten in his basket. Mum and Dad looked at each other in surprise. She usually argued about everything! They both relaxed and smiled at Tara. Suddenly she felt a warm fuzzy happy feeling inside.

After lunch Mel sulked. No one had ever seen her pout before. "It's not fair you get a kitten," she muttered darkly. And Jack ran round and round the house shouting, "I'm going to get a puppy. I'm going to get a dog of my very own."

Tara was just going to scream back, "No you're not. Ha! Ha!" in her nasty voice but Ash-ting looked at her with his big green eyes and she kept quiet.

"Can I hold him?" wheedled Mel.

"He's my kitten," shouted Tara and was about to add, "so no you can't," when she felt the strange feeling in her forehead again.

"Stop it Tara. Of course she can hold me," said Ash-ting.

Reluctantly Tara handed him over. She watched anxiously as he settled in Mel's arms, purring loudly as she stroked him. What if he loved her sister more than her? Tara felt a horrid feeling in her stomach and she wanted to grab Ash-ting back.

Almost immediately she felt what was becoming a familiar buzz in her forehead and she heard, *"I'm your kitten, Tara."* She looked over at her lovely new kitten lying in her sister's arms and smiled like she hadn't smiled in a long time.

Tara felt her life would never be the same again, but she did not know quite how much it would change.

Auntie Dottie comes back

At six o'clock the front door bell rang. The family looked at each other in surprise – they weren't expecting anybody else to visit. The children raced to the door, followed by their parents. It was Auntie Dottie again, still wearing the red spotted dress and carrying her huge bag. Tara felt herself shrivel. She saw that Auntie Dottie was holding two big tubes of sweets and she just knew one would be for Jack and one for Mel. Her throat felt as if she had swallowed stinging nettles. She cuddled Ash-ting and tried not to cry.

They all went into the sitting room. She wanted to hang back but Ash-ting purred and she realized he wanted her to go with the others.

"It will be alright," he purred. *"Is there anything you like about your Auntie's dress, just one nice thing?"*

Tara thought for a while and then silently answered: "Yes, I like the big brooch she's wearing with the red shiny stones."

"Then smile at her and tell her you like it," said Ash-ting.

Encouraged by Ash-ting's words Tara swallowed down the scratchy feeling in her throat and summoned up as sunny a smile as she could.

"Auntie Dottie, I love your brooch. It's all pretty and shiny," she said. And then a strange thing happened. Auntie Dottie smiled back. She looked down at the two tubes of sweets and reached into her bag for a third one for Tara. Tara felt a smile in her chest.

"Thank you Auntie Dottie. Would you like to stroke Ash-ting?"

Auntie Dottie took the kitten and stroked him. Ash-ting purred loudly when she touched him. "He likes you," volunteered Tara and her aunt looked soft and friendly.

Then another miracle took place. Auntie Dottie handed the kitten back to Tara and

rummaged in her bag, pulling out a big oblong box wrapped in coloured paper.

"Perhaps I was a bit hasty this morning, Happy Birthday Tara." Tara opened the box and took out the singing doll she had so much wanted.

"Oh thank you Auntie Dottie," she exclaimed. With the doll in one hand and Ash-ting in the other arm, she somehow managed to give her auntie a big hug. Little zings of delight jumped about inside her.

Before bed time, as Tara was playing in her bedroom with her doll and Ash-ting, she whispered to him, "Thank you Ash-ting, this has been my best birthday ever because of you."

He yawned. *"Thank you too Tara and well done. I told you what to do – but you did it."*

Monday morning

Tara hated going to school, especially on Monday mornings. This week was worse than ever. She didn't want to leave Ash-ting. She dawdled and argued until her mother was exasperated.

"I've got to go to work to earn some money while Jack's at pre-school. You know that!" She was used to hearing how they didn't have enough money.

"Yeah," she said and continued to play with Ash-ting.

Jack didn't help. "I'll play with the kitten when I get home from pre-school," he taunted. Tara flew at him in rage and grabbed his sweater. Jack yelled loudly. She was about to hit him when she felt a loud ping in her forehead. *"No Tara! No!"* She stopped. Ash-ting ran up to her and innocently rubbed against her legs. She let go of Jack's sweater and picked up the kitten.

"Stop and think Tara. Why is Jack winding you up?" Ash-ting asked.

Tara was thoughtful for a moment.

"Is it because he's jealous?" she asked.

"That's right. I'm your kitten and he wishes he had a kitten or a puppy. Can you afford to be generous?"

"I suppose so," she whispered.

Ash-ting's big green eyes watched her steadily as she turned to talk to a worried looking Jack.

"It will be nice for Ash-ting to have someone to play with," said Tara in a much softer voice than usual.

Jack stared at her in surprise. "Thanks Tara," he whooped with delight.

When her Mum came in to see what the rumpus was about, the two children were friends.

Was she imaging things – or did she just see Tara's new kitten smile?

For the first time ever Tara laughed happily and danced out the door on her way to school. Mel and Jack walked nicely by their mother. Tara skipped.

She could see Tracy ahead. She lived in their street and was in her class. She had fair curls and big brown eyes and Tara wanted to be her friend. But, not surprisingly, Tracy would not play with her because Tara would not share her toys and – even worse – had once pulled her hair. When Tara complained that she had no one to play with her mother was unsympathetic. "It's your own fault," she responded. "You have to be nice to people for them to want to play with you." But Tara didn't know how to be nice.

Tracy was best friends with Rebecca and they went everywhere together. Perhaps today would be different, thought Tara, but when she entered the playground she saw Tracy and Rebecca running towards each other. Tara stood by herself, again.

She noticed that Rosy was standing alone, too. She was new at school and no-one played with her because she had a squint. Suddenly she felt a buzz in her forehead and wondered if it was Ash-ting: could he talk to her from a distance?

"Of course I can. And I can see you. All cats are psychic!"

"What does that mean?"

"We can see and hear things most humans can't. Now go and talk to Rosy, she's lonely."

"But I don't like her. She's got funny eyes."

"She's a nice, gentle little girl and you can help her. Go and say hello."

Tara looked at the lonely little girl as if she had never seen her before. Her hair was brown and straight and she looked scared and droopy. Tara had never tried to help anyone before but she trusted Ash-ting. She walked over to where Rosy was standing all alone.

"Hello Rosy," she said. "I got a new kitten for my birthday and a singing doll."

"Oh!" said the child, looking surprised that someone had spoken to her. "How lovely. What's your kitten like?"

"He's grey all over and he purrs and he...." She stopped quickly. She had been going to blurt out that he talked to her, but decided that was probably best kept a secret – at least for now. "…and his name is Ash-ting."

"Oh I'd love an animal," said Rosy sadly. "We used to have a dog but…"

"But what?" asked Tara.

"But my Mummy and Daddy have split up and we had to move to a little flat. Daddy's got Goldie but I'm not allowed to see him." She said this in a small sad voice and Tara felt sorry for her.

"Would you like to come and play with Ash-ting after school, if your Mummy will let you?"

Rosy's face lit up.

"I'd love to…." Then her face fell again as she seemed to remember something. "But I have to go to my Grandad's after school and get his tea."

Tara didn't know what to say. Her Mummy made tea for her and Jack and Mel every day. And she had Ash-ting, her very own kitten. The bell rang and they went into the classroom.

At break time Tara went over to Tracy and Rebecca. As soon as they saw her, they held hands and turned their backs on her, making it quite clear they did not want to play.

"Take no notice. Tell them about me," buzzed Ash-ting.

"I've got a new kitten," she said. Her voice was so happy and excited that they turned towards her and asked curiously what he was like. Tara told them everything – except her special secret.

"You can come to my house to see him if you like."

They looked at each other then back at Tara again.

"Will you let us play with him?'

"Yes, you can stroke him and cuddle him. And you can play with my new singing doll."

The two girls spoke in unison, "Then you can be our friend."

Rebecca held Tara's hand and Tara felt very happy.
Tara looked round and saw Rosy watching them. She looked very unhappy and Tara wanted to ignore her. She was friends with Tracy and Rebecca now. But she felt a thumping on her forehead and knew Ash-ting was somehow watching her. She told Tracy and Rebecca she would just be a moment and ran over to Rosy. "Come and play with us," she said. Rosy's face lit up with a smile that made her look beautiful. They ran back and Tara took Rebecca's hand again. Rebecca smiled. Tracy smiled and Tara laughed out loud with joy. At last she had friends!

On the way home from school Tara told her Mum all about Tracy and Rebecca and asked if they could come and play one day. She agreed to phone their mothers to see if they could come round after school on Tuesday. "But you've got to be nice to them," she warned and Tara felt a cross feeling in her chest. Then she remembered Ash-ting and relaxed. She was sure her kitten would help her. She chattered on about Rosy, how she had bad eyes, how her parents had split up and she couldn't see her Dad or her dog, and she had to live in a flat and go to make tea for her grandfather every day after school. "Poor little girl!" exclaimed her mother but nothing more was said. It made Tara feel sad when she talked about Rosy.

But Rosy was forgotten when they arrived home and Ash-ting ran to meet her at the door with his tail up in the air.

"Hello Tara. You did really well at school today."

"Thank you," she whispered back to him.

Jack and Mel were out on play dates so Tara was by herself. For once she didn't mind, because now she had Ash-ting she was never really on her own. They sat on the lawn together with her juice and a biscuit and Tara played happily with her singing doll. She told Ash-ting about Rosy and her sad life.

"You can help her. You have already started to help by including her in your games. You must do the same again tomorrow."

"But Tracy and Rebecca are my friends now. They might not want her to play again tomorrow," Tara looked stricken.

"Tara when you are kind to people things have a way of working out." Ash-ting put his paw on her arm, and Tara somehow trusted what he said.

Daddy needs help

Later that evening something much more serious happened and Tara forgot all about Rosy and her problems.

Her mother was impatient. She was waiting for Dad to come home from work, so she could go out and work her shift at the supermarket. "There's never enough money and you need new shoes again," she said crossly to Tara – as if it was her fault.

At that moment Dad came in and her Mum rushed out without even looking at him. Her father looked terrible. His face was full of worry. He walked straight into the sitting room without saying 'Hello' and shut the door.

Tara knew something was the matter, but what could she do? She felt an icy scared feeling. Her tummy was tight and she wanted to scream. She opened her mouth to howl and Ash-ting put his paw up to her lips.

"No! No! Hush Tara. Calm down."

"But Daddy didn't even speak to me or Mummy," she wailed. "He doesn't love me any more. They'll split up like Rosy's parents and they both won't want me, they are always cross with me."

"Both your parents love you very much, but your Daddy has a big problem right now and you can help him."

"Me! Help Daddy. How? I'm just a little girl," she sobbed.

"Tara, do you love your Daddy?"

"Yes of course," she replied startled.

"Then do what I say. OK?"

She nodded.

"Go quietly into the sitting room and ask him what's bothering him?"

"I can't. He'll say nothing's wrong or that I'm just a little girl and can't understand," she protested.

"You will be fine and I will be with you. Now go along"

"Alright," replied Tara, "but only if you really come in with me."

She walked over to the door and turned the handle bravely. Dad looked up and gave her a grave half smile. She sat by him on the sofa.

"What's wrong, Dad?" she asked in a gentle voice. Ash-ting rubbed against his legs and he gave him a half-hearted stroke.

"You wouldn't understand. You're just a little girl."

Tara looked at Ash-ting with an 'I told you so!' look on her face.

"Say you love him and you know something's the matter." Ash-ting hopped up onto her father's lap and Tara did as she was asked, watching her Dad with big concerned eyes.

"I made a mistake at work and I am worried I'll lose my job when my boss finds out," he sighed, looking sadder than she had ever seen him.

Tara nodded, though she could feel her hands cold with fear. Mum always said she didn't know what they'd do if he lost his job.

"Tell him to phone his boss now and talk to him," said Ash-ting.

Tara took a deep breath and once again did as Ash-ting told her, adding: "You always say honesty is best Dad."

Tara's Dad looked at her in surprise.

"You're right. Of course you are. I'll do it right now. Go out and play in the garden. I'll be out in ten minutes."

Tara sat on the swing, hugging Ash-ting. She felt like they sat there for ever. Fifteen minutes later Daddy came out smiling.

"You were quite right little one. My boss said everyone makes mistakes and we could sort it out. He said it was a good thing I told him so promptly."

"Hooray," said Tara, high-fiving her Dad.

"Come one, you deserve an ice cream," he said, hugging her as he lifted her from the swing.

Tara and her Daddy sat happily in the garden enjoying their ice creams. Ash-ting suggested Tara should ask her Daddy what he used to like doing when he was a child.

He looked dreamy for a while, then said: "I loved to draw, especially animals. I really wanted to be an artist but my parents said it wasn't a proper job. That's why I work in an office doing accounts. I do miss drawing though."

Ash-ting sat up and licked his fur.

"Oh Daddy, would you draw Ash-ting for me?"

"It's a long time since I've done any drawing, but I'll have a go."

Together they fetched some paper and pencils and Tara's Dad did a wonderful sketch of Ash-ting.

"It's great, thank you Dad. I'll take it to school tomorrow to show everyone – look Ash-ting, it's you."

She held her new picture up in front of her kitten and he seemed to purr appreciatively.

Tuesday

Everyone at school thought the picture of Ashting was beautiful. "I wish my Dad could draw like that," Tracy said and Tara glowed with pleasure. Mrs. Smith, their teacher, put it up on the wall, where everyone could see it. Tara was beginning to enjoy school more and more.

After school Tracy and Rebecca came to play.

"Tara, remember you've got to let them play with your toys, and with me" Ash-ting buzzed her as the girls walked home together. *"You have to follow through on promises."*

'I will,' she agreed. And she did.

The girls had a lovely time and Tracy and Rebecca said they had really enjoyed playing with her. It was the next best day to her birthday.

Wednesday

"It seems almost too good to be true," murmured Mummy to Daddy next morning. "Tara's like a different child. That kitten's had a good influence."

Sadly it was too good to be true. After breakfast Jack grabbed Tara's doll and ran off with it, taunting her. Tara was enraged. She rushed at Jack screaming and smacked him really hard as they fought over her doll. Tara yelled and rained blows on her little brother. When her Mum tried to stop her, she attacked her too. Her fury was out of control. She could hear Ash-ting in her forehead telling her to stop but she just couldn't.

When her Mum eventually managed to drag Tara off Jack, she refused to apologize.

"It was his fault," she shouted, red in the face.

"Yes," said Mummy patiently "and Jack has said sorry for taking your doll, but you must say sorry for hitting him,"

Tara would not apologize. Eventually Mummy locked the screaming Tara in her room. Then she comforted Jack, who was the one who had pinched her doll. The doll lay with a torn dress on the floor.

"It's so unfair," shouted the little girl as she lay on her bed. "I hate Jack and I hate Mummy." The whole household was upset.

"It's just like it used to be," Mum sighed "and just when I thought things were getting better."

"They are," said Dad, thinking of the child who had talked to him in such a grown up way the other day. "I think it's just a blip."

"I hope you're right," replied Mum. "And why are you looking so cheerful this morning?"

"I did a drawing the other day for Tara," said Dad, "and it has got me thinking, I really enjoyed it and I might start doing some more art work."

"Well don't get carried away. Remember we have three children to support." Dad could feel a little grey cloud of sadness form over him again.

Ash-ting watched it all.

At the school gate that morning Mummy gave
Tara an extra hug and a kiss and said, "I love
you. I just don't like the way you behave."

But Tara knew it wasn't true. No one really loved her – except Ash-ting. She was cross and miserable all morning and when she wanted to play with Tracy and Rebecca at break time they didn't want to play with her. Rosy wasn't at school that day, she had a hospital appointment, so Tara stood in the playground all alone thinking how unfair life was. She felt the buzz in her forehead and knew Ash-ting wanted to talk, but she felt so out-of-sorts she even ignored him.

The Aura

After lunch she felt a bit better and next time Ash-ting buzzed she listened in as he said, *"Cheer up. Tracy and Rebecca still want to play with you — just not when you are grumpy."*

Tara felt a spark of hope in her chest and smiled, because she trusted Ash-ting.

"That's better, now your aura is pink again your friends will want to play with you."

"What's an aura?" asked Tara, feeling even happier now — even though she did not know what Ash-ting meant.

"You aura is the light around you. People can sense it even if they can't see it. It was black when you were cross so no one wanted to be near you. Now it is pink, they will. Go and play."

Tara ran over to Tracy and Rebecca and joined in their game as if nothing had ever been wrong.

"If you do something good for someone it always comes back to you, maybe from someone else," Ash-ting told Tara.

"Really!" exclaimed Tara, fascinated and surprised.

"Absolutely," the kitten nodded his head.

"So the more nice things I do the more nice things will happen to me?" Tara checked.

"Yes. But you've got to be genuinely nice – not pretend nice."

"OK. I'm going to do a nice thing every day," the little girl decided happily and she started thinking of a list of kind or good actions.

Ash-ting was pleased to see how cheerful she looked. *"I know where you could start. How about something that would make your Daddy happy?"*

Tara skipped off to find her Daddy.

"Daddy, are you going to be helping with the school fete next week?"

"Of course," he replied. "I usually do the hoop-la stall."

"But Daddy everybody would love it if you did drawings," suggested Tara, her eyes shining. "You could draw pets from photos and even some of the children. I bet everyone would want one and it would raise lots of money for the school. You said you really enjoy drawing."

Dad hesitated for a moment – yes he did love drawing, but would his drawings really be good enough for the school fete? Tara looked so eager and happy; he didn't want to let her down.

"What a great idea Tara, fancy you thinking of that. Yes, I will do it if the school wants me to. I will talk to them tomorrow."

"Thank you Daddy." She gave him a big hug.

Rosy's Mum

Tara's mother was working in the supermarket that evening. It was very quiet. A tall thin woman came to her check out. She unloaded her trolley and asked: "Are you Tara's mother?"

"Yes," agreed Tara's Mum cautiously, wondering what her daughter had said or done wrong now. But the lady smiled.

"I'm Rosy Farthing's mother. Your daughter has really helped Rosy to settle in at her new school. Tara's been very kind. Rosy is very shy because of her bad eye and Tara has helped her to make friends."

"Oh thank you. That's nice to hear," Tara's mother was pink with pleasure. "How did the hospital appointment go? Tara said Rosy went for a check today."

"Very well, thank you. She's going back again next week and they should be able to do something to help with her eye – it will be a wonderful birthday present for her."

Tara's mother explained that Tara was eager for Rosy to come and play one day after school and asked if she would like to do it on her birthday as a special treat?

Rosy's mother looked embarrassed.

"Thank you. That's very kind of you, but her birthday is Saturday, the day of the school fete. And she can't really play after school, you see my father's in a wheelchair and he's rather lonely and since there's no one to look after Rosy when school finishes she goes there every day."

"I see. It must be difficult for you on your own."

"Yes it is." Rosy's mother looked tired and very sad.

"And it's hard on a child not to see her Dad or her dog," murmured Tara's Mum.

Mrs. Farthing's face snapped tight like a door slamming. "It's best that she doesn't see them," she said, picked up her bags quickly and left.

Tara's Mummy relayed the conversation she'd had with Rosy Farthing's mother to her husband later that evening.

"What a shame," he sighed. "There's a man called Ron Farthing at work, I wonder if he's Rosy's Dad? Quiet fellow. He looks very unhappy these days. I believe he lives with his mother in the pink house on the hill – the one with the big oak tree in the front garden."

"Oh yes, I know the house," said Mummy. "Her Dad's looking after their dog and Rosy's missing both of them," she sighed and wondered if there was anything she could do.

"Best not to interfere," warned Dad.

"No, you're right," agreed Mum. "It's not our business. There's nothing we can do."

But Tara was sitting under the kitchen table listening and she had different ideas. So did Ash-ting. They slipped out into the garden and Tara sat on the swing with the kitten on her knee.

"What can we do to help Rosy?" she whispered.

Thursday

Ash-ting made a plan which filled Tara with excitement. She had to ask Mel to help because she was nine and could write very well. In exchange Tara had to promise to do all Mel's jobs for a week and let her friends play with Ash-ting. Mel wrote a secret letter:

> Dear Rosy's Daddy,
> Please come to our school fete on
> Saturday at 4 o'clock with a picture of
> your doggy so my Daddy can draw
> him for Rosy's birthday present.
> Love from Tara.

They addressed the envelope to

> Mr. Farthing, (Rosy's Daddy)
> The pink house on the hill,
> With the big oak tree in the front garden
> Urgent please.

Friday

Rosy had an operation on her eye on Friday and did not come to school. Tara hoped she would be at the school fete. The whole class drew get well cards for Rosy. Tara drew four little girls holding hands and wrote four names below them: Tara, Rosy, Tracy and Rebecca. She wanted Rosy to know she had some friends to come back to at school.

Saturday

Dad was whistling as he shaved on Saturday morning. It was the day of the fete and he was looking forward to doing the drawings to raise funds for the school. Jack was happy because his picture had been chosen to go on the classroom wall and Mel was excited about her part in the dance display. Tara was excited and nervous – would Rosy's Dad come along?

Jack was happy because his picture had been chosen to go on the classroom wall. He held Mummy's hand as he pulled her into the classroom. Proudly he pointed out his drawing of a blue train on red rails. Automatically Tara was about to say, "Yuk what a stupid picture," when she felt a buzz sent by Ash-ting. *"Find one nice thing to say about Jack's painting, Tara. One nice thing."* She stopped to think. "I like the colour of the train, Jack," she commented. He beamed. Mum and Dad smiled and everyone was happy.

They watched Mel in her dancing display and Tara clapped louder than anyone.

After that Dad went to his table to start the drawings. There was such a long queue that they had to make appointments and the afternoon was soon fully booked right up to 3.30. Tracy's mother was trying to persuade him to draw her dog. Dad shook his head, his day was fully booked. Tara was in a panic. She was sure that Tracy's Mum would insist that he do it at four o'clock, but Dad was supposed to finish by then.

"Dad, please I want you to paint Rosy's dog for her birthday," blurted Tara, "I promised you'd do it at 4 o'clock when your appointments were finished."

"Of course, but I can always draw her dog another time," smiled Dad. He was in a good humour, doing what he loved to do.

"No Dad, it's her birthday today!"

Seeing how much this meant to his daughter, he agreed with Tracy's Mum to take the photo of her dog home and draw it for her that evening. Tara breathed a sigh of relief.

But where was Rosy? And had her Dad even got the letter? Tara was beginning to feel very nervous about her plan. Rosy and her Mum arrived at half past three. Tara squealed with excitement and ran over to wish her friend a 'Happy Birthday'. Rosy beamed – she was wearing a patch over one eye and Jack said she looked like a pirate. They all laughed.

"Mummy, why don't you and Mrs. Farthing go for a cup of tea," Tara suggested, "while Rosy and I watch Daddy drawing. Shall we Rosy?" She smiled persuasively at Rosy and took hold of her hand. Rosy looked at her Mum for permission.

"Alright, as long as Tara's Dad doesn't mind," she agreed. Their mothers took Jack with them on the promise of an ice cream. For once Tara was not interested in ice cream!

The two girls ran over to sit on the grass by Tara's Dad.

"What time is it Daddy?" Tara asked.

"Ten to four," he said with a smile. He wondered if Rosy knew he was to draw her dog. "I am running a little late," he warned. At ten past four he handed a sketch of a rabbit to a young boy who was delighted with it. Tara felt terrible. Rosy's Dad wasn't coming. She knew it. Dad looked at her and winked.

"And now Tara, what did you want me to draw?" She couldn't speak. Her throat was too tight. It was all going wrong.

Rosy's Dad

Then suddenly there was a commotion. A dark haired man with a huge dog on a lead was running through the crowd looking very anxious. Then he saw Rosy and his face broke into the biggest smile, "Oh Rosy, my birthday girl."

Rosy jumped up and screamed. "Daddy! It's my Daddy! And Goldie."

Then she and her Dad were hugging as if they would never let go and Goldie was leaping all over them barking.

The two girls' mothers were walking across the field back towards them as all the commotion was taking place. They stopped and stared. Rosy's Mum had a tense look on her face. Rosy's Dad turned and looked at Tara, "You must be Tara. I only just got the letter. It went next door! I've raced here and thought I'd probably missed you girls."

They all looked at each other. What letter?
Tara said nothing. Dad looked at her and
guessed what she had done. He put his arm
round her and hugged her close.

Rosy's mother did not even look at her husband. She put her hand out to Rosy who reluctantly moved away from her father's embrace and obediently took her mother's hand. They walked away in silence. Rosy's Dad called out after her, "Happy Birthday sweetheart, I love you Rosy."

Rosy turned for a moment and whispered, "I love you too Daddy."

Goldie whimpered.

Tara's mother invited Mr. Farthing and Goldie back to their house for a cup of tea. Daddy said he would draw a picture of Goldie when they were at home. Mr. Farthing was very grateful and said he would put it in an envelope and take it straight round to Rosy's flat so that she got it on her birthday. Ash-ting was waiting on the doorstep and Tara took him into the garden to tell him what had happened. She had a feeling he knew already but he listened gravely.

"You can't make two adults love each other," he told her. *"But they do both love Rosy."*

"I just wish she could see her Dad and Goldie."

"You have done everything with the best intentions, so perhaps it will work out. Let's wait and see," purred Ash-ting as Tara crossed her fingers and tickled him behind his ears.

Daddy drew the most beautiful picture of Goldie but he wouldn't take any money for it. The dog looked as if he was ready to jump out of the page.

Mummy was extremely impressed and said to him: "I think you should do more pictures, everyone loves them and you could earn some extra money selling them."

They all laughed, especially Daddy, who hugged Mummy in delight.

Mr. Farthing left to deliver Rosy's card. An hour later there was a knock at the door and they all rushed to answer it. To their surprise Rosy stood there with her Daddy and Goldie. Rosy was holding a bunch of flowers. She held them out to Tara's Dad and whispered, "Thank you for the picture, it was lovely."

Her Dad was smiling. He explained that Rosy had seen him going up the driveway to post her card and had come running out to meet him. Rosy's mother was still angry, but Rosy kept saying that all she wanted for her birthday was to see her Daddy.

"Then Goldie went bounding over and licked Rosy's mother. It's funny," he added. "She seemed to change then. It was like magic, she agreed to let Rosy come out for a walk with me for an hour. It's a beginning."

"Come in for a minute," said Mummy. She put seven candles on a cake for Rosy and they all sang Happy Birthday to her. Then she blew out the candles and made a wish – though Tara guessed her wish had already come true. She was very shy and pink. Afterwards they waved goodbye as Rosy skipped down the path holding her Daddy's hand while Goldie ran ahead.

Bedtime

When Tara was tucked up in bed that night she snuggled up to Ash-ting. "I love you Ash-ting. Thank you for being my friend. You're right," she murmured sleepily, "When I'm nice people do like me and things do have a way of working out when you help other people. It also feels really good."

Ash-ting purred a sleepy purr and sent a secret thank you to Goldie for playing his part in their plan.

In the same collection...

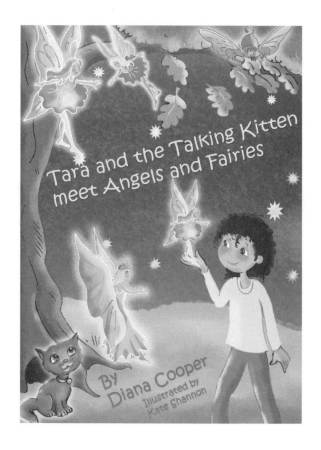

Tara and the Talking Kitten
meet Angels and Fairies

By
Diana Cooper

Illustrated by
Kate Shannon

and more to come!